The rancher who saved Christmas

Justice Willoughby

CHAPTER 1

With Christmas just days away, the Wyoming wind grew fiercer, carrying a chill that seemed to cut to the bone. A snowstorm was imminent. The sky had turned a dull, heavy grey, foretelling more snow. Edwin Parker watched it from the large window of his office at "Aspen Creek Deliveries", steam rising from his coffee cup blending with his breath. Meanwhile, the scent of wrapping paper, duct tape, and freshly brewed coffee filled the air.

The clock on the wall read 7:38 a.m., but he had been there for over an hour. Just like every day, especially in the past few weeks. The build-up to Christmas was always like this; he'd grown used to the hustle and bustle and had resigned himself to enduring it as long as necessary.

Edwin was thirty-two years old and had a habit, formed since adolescence, of beginning his day well before dawn, when all was still quiet and the world seemed to demand nothing of him. Thanks to a healthy exercise routine he'd kept up since his days as a nearly professional baseball player, he preserved his lean figure and upright shoulders, as if his posture masked the weight he carried inside. His brown hair always fell slightly too long over his forehead, and despite his daily efforts to keep it in place, it ended up looking dishevelled again. A bit like everything else in his life.

His eyes, a warm hazel, held the quiet light of someone who observes the world more than they wish to speak. There was kindness in his gaze, but also a lingering melancholy, a subtle weariness that stemmed not from the pressure of work, but from a deeper, more personal source.

Meanwhile, on the wooden benches surrounding him, day after day, dozens of packages piled up. Some bore handwritten notes: *"A thought for you, with love"*, *"Don't open before Christmas"*, *"Best wishes, my love"*. It was always fascinating to try to discern the personality of the sender and the recipient, as well as the nature of their relationship.

Every time he skimmed through them, even absentmindedly, Edwin felt a small lump tighten in his throat. These were the lives of others, their expectations, their carefully packaged affections. He was merely the conduit.

He sighed, shook his head, and refocused on the delivery list. He couldn't afford any distractions; he had no time to waste! The pressure was already mounting with the looming deadlines.

'Shipments to the areas bordering Pine Hollow, Red Valley, and Meadow Creek are still pending,' he muttered to himself, scribbling neat lines on his tablet. 'Damn, I have to get this done! No matter what.'

Christmas Eve was just four days away, and the workload seemed to increase relentlessly by the hour. It was as if every Aspen Creek resident depended on him to deliver gifts and packages to their destinations, even to the most remote ranches in the area, where cell phone service was patchy, and the roads threatened to turn into sheets of ice.

'Edwin always gets it right,' everyone in town said. 'Entrusting Edwin with a delivery is a sure bet. Edwin never lets us down!'

Only he knew how much effort and stress the "fame" he had built over the years cost him.

The bell above the door rang, and Tyler, his young helper, entered, rubbing his arms to keep warm.

'Damn, it's so cold!' he snorted, stamping his feet on the floor to shake the snow off his boots. Then he took off his wool hat, running a hand through his blond hair. 'Did you hear the forecast, Ed? They say the storm of the year is coming. In fact, of the years. Maybe even of the century.'

Edwin offered him a half-smile, the one he always used to ease tension.

'Yes, I've heard, but don't worry. You know they always say that, every year around this time. And each time, they exaggerate.'

'I know, but everyone's saying it this time,' Tyler insisted, blowing on his hands. 'My grandma put extra blankets on the beds. If she's getting ready, too, it means it's going to be tough. She usually doesn't make mistakes! And my shoulder might be a sign of something, too; it's bothering me more than usual today.'

'So, you need to stop pushing yourself, Tyler, or you'll never feel better! That's what it's trying to tell you. Listen to your shoulder if you don't want to obey the doctor.'

Tyler Johnston, despite his young age, was a valuable assistant to him. Unfortunately, he had injured himself during his last football practice. Although the boy underestimated the situation, Edwin never wanted him to cause further harm.

'It was just a pulled muscle. I'm definitely not going to stop because of this. My shoulder has no say in the matter; it needs to learn to obey and stop complaining.'

Edwin forced a smile, but deep inside, anxiety took shape and grew more pressing. Tyler was a strong and determined boy, but he certainly couldn't risk his health. In any case, it wasn't just the storm that worried him, but mostly the thought of not being able to deliver everything. Of disappointing someone. He hated the idea of letting down the people who trusted him.

It had always been like this in his life: duty before anything else.

Work had been his main refuge since his relationship with Marvin ended three years earlier. When the man he'd loved for nearly a decade decided that life in a mountain town was no longer suitable for him, Edwin didn't resist. He didn't shout or plead, fully aware that it would be embarrassing and, above all, pointless. Instead, he closed himself off, like a window during a storm. He accepted his decision and let him go. Only later did Edwin discover that Marvin, even before moving permanently to Las Vegas to start a new restaurant venture, had been manipulating and cheating on him for some time with the man who would later become his new partner in life and work. Marvin's abandonment was, in effect, premeditated; he was simply waiting to take everything he could from him.

Since then, work had become more than just a task; it was his armour, his home. His salvation. It hadn't been easy to surrender to reality, but no longer relying on people and relationships had become part of his approach to life, day by day.

Meanwhile, the day continued in a whirlwind of activity, almost without pause: the van needed loading, deliveries had to be made, packages needed to be registered, calls had to be answered. Outside, the snow started to fall gradually but increasingly heavily, an unstoppable process that would prevent him from catching up on lost time.

Tyler had assisted him for a few hours with the delivery records, but then Edwin had almost insisted that he go home and rest. The boy had complained, but Edwin was absolutely determined not to risk him injuring himself and hindering his recovery.

Around noon, Madyson Thornton, the mayor of Aspen Creek, peered into the Aspen Creek Deliveries office. She was a cheerful and lively woman, dressed in a bright red coat and a matching wool hat with a large bobble, a reflection of her love for knitting. Her attire was always quite eccentric, in summer and winter, so much so that she never went unnoticed.

'Edwin, dear!' she exclaimed, bringing with her a blast of chilly air and the scent of cinnamon cookies she was craving. 'You're already at your limit, aren't you? I spoke to your mother last night at our knitting and crochet class. Janet's really worried about you; she says you'll end up sick if you carry on like this. I mean, you don't even have time to answer the phone!'

Edwin smirked and rolled his eyes before rolling up his sleeves. There was no denying the evidence, especially since he stood no chance against the knitting and crochet class his mother and Madyson were attending.

'Yes, Madyson, I'm quite close to my limit. But we'll get through this, as always. Don't worry, I'm doing fine! My mum's overreacting, as usual. I answer the phone, though.'

Madyson gazed at him with that look of hers that combined affection and concern.

'I know you'll make it, and I also know you never hold back. But you can't do it all alone, dear. Especially this time, with Tyler injured. And then, there's the storm approaching, and you'll need strong, healthy hands. So I'll ask someone to give you a hand.'

'Someone?'

Edwin raised an eyebrow. Why did people always have the habit of meddling? He was perfectly capable of doing his job alone! He'd been doing it for years now.

'Exactly, my dear.'

Madyson nodded with a sly look; she was skilled at keeping people on edge. She was piquing his curiosity, despite everything, to the point that he felt compelled to surrender.

'All right! To whom?'

'To Chase Lewis. You know him, don't you?'

The name echoed through his mind like a gust of wind. Of course, Edwin knew him by sight. After all, who didn't know Chase Lewis in Aspen Creek? He was the owner of the "Silver Pine" ranch, a somewhat rough man, a man of few words and many actions. But he was also a man who mostly kept to himself and wasn't often seen in town. Some called him "the lone hero" after the year before he had saved two children trapped in the frozen river, risking death from exposure. Others, however, found him difficult, stubborn, and perpetually sulky. He didn't particularly enjoy interacting with other people, so as not to feel pressured to justify his choices, and he kept his distance, considering that the ranch was his life and he seemed to care about nothing else.

In a way, Edwin could relate to him. Recently, it was the same for him as well. Work was everything, the pivotal point around which his entire life revolved. He had neither time nor inclination for anything else.

'I thank you, but I don't believe it's necessary...'

He didn't dare admit it to Madyson, but the thought of dealing with that attractive yet reserved man made him uneasy. And Edwin despised feeling uneasy. For him, it was like a warning sign, a sense of "danger" he didn't want to fall into again.

Edwin would have liked to do his best to dissuade the mayor, but she immediately silenced him with a wave of her hand.

'I won't take no for an answer. Chase will be coming into town to pick up some supplies for his ranch, and he's already said he'll need to come back often over the next few days. You'll definitely need help when the roads get blocked, trust me. And he, besides being very strong, knows how to handle snowstorms.'

'What makes you think Chase Lewis will agree to help me?'

'The fact that he usually tries to lend a hand when someone is in trouble. He's a good guy. Trust me, I've known him for a long time.'

Edwin nodded, more out of politeness than conviction. He didn't like delegating or relying on anyone. Too often, people promised to help him but backed out and walked away, leaving him to his fate. This feeling increasingly disheartened and frustrated him. As a result, his distrust of others had grown immeasurably.

By the time evening fell over Aspen Creek, the snow had covered everything like a silent white quilt. The Christmas lights on the houses flickered among the flakes, and the distant sound of a radio played old Christmas carols, regularly broadcast around the same time each year.

Around ten o'clock that evening, Edwin closed the warehouse door and paused for a moment in the doorway, his hands in his pockets and his breath hanging in the still air. The town of Aspen Creek, at that hour, was so quiet it seemed asleep. Only the loud roar of the wind shattered the silence.

He looked out at the deserted street and wondered, for a moment, what it would be like to go home and find someone waiting for him. Someone who would say:

"Forget about work for now, come here and tell me about your day."

He snorted and shook his head, nearly annoyed by how his thoughts had wandered. They pulled him straight back to Marvin and his betrayal, to the planning of a new life he had decided not to include him in. Solitude was much easier, from Edwin's perspective, and above all, much safer.

But as he locked the gate and prepared to get into his old pickup truck, he heard a notification on his phone. He reached into his jacket pocket and opened it; it was a text from Madyson.

"I'll send Chase Lewis to you tomorrow morning. Don't argue, let me help you for once! Good night, dear. M."

Edwin sighed and slipped his mobile back into his jacket. Fine, he wouldn't argue. It wouldn't be worth it with Madyson Thornton, anyway; he knew her too well. Since he was a child, she had been an old friend of his mother's.

Meanwhile, the sky above Aspen Creek had darkened completely, and the first proper snowstorm of winter was looming on the horizon. Tyler's grandmother was right; this year would be worse than previous ones. But it had to be faced, somehow.

Deep down, Edwin knew it wasn't just snow that was approaching. It was something, or someone, fated to disturb the perfect order of his life or, more specifically, his monotonous daily routine. If he'd allowed it.

CHAPTER 2

The snow had fallen all night, soft yet firm, nearly covering the driveways, gates, and mailboxes around Aspen Creek. The morning silence was broken only by the crunch of boots sinking into the snow and the warm breath of horses, which puffed out clouds of steam in the biting cold.

Chase Lewis ran a hand over his chin and rough beard, looking up at the sky, which, he was sure, promised more snow. More snow that would be heavier and more persistent. It wouldn't leave many options except to accept it and stay hunkered down, waiting for it to stop. The wind stung his face, but he was used to all that. Just as he was now accustomed to understanding and interpreting the weather conditions that would prevail in that part of Wyoming.

For Chase, the cold wasn't an enemy to fight, but an old friend with whom he had formed a kind of pact. He was born and raised in that tough land, surrounded by untended fences and frozen fields. Over thirty-five years, he had learned that nature cannot be controlled but must be respected. Only then can one live alongside it and sometimes even learn something valuable.

His ranch, "Silver Pine", stretched out before and behind him. It was a vast expanse of pasture and coniferous forest, with a splendid brick house, clad in walnut-coloured wood, and a large barn with a red roof. It was the house that had always belonged to his parents, who had died in a car accident about fifteen years earlier, when he was still a boy. Thus, in addition to the property, they had also left him a legacy of debts and responsibilities that he had always underestimated and left to others to manage. Since then, Chase had worked hard to rebuild everything: the animals, the facilities, but above all, his balance and emotional stability. At the same time, he had also worked hard on himself to understand who he was and what he wanted from life.

Even physically, he had become the very embodiment of stability. Or, more precisely, solidity: very tall and muscular, with broad shoulders, large, powerful hands, and a square face marked by small wrinkles at the corners of his steel-grey eyes. He had adopted the gait of someone used to walking with ease through mud and snow, with the deep, slightly hoarse voice of someone who has learned to speak only when necessary to break the silence.

Yet beneath his frontiersman-like appearance, a subtle sadness lingered inside him that only those who truly knew him could notice. For nearly a year, Chase had lived alone. After Davis left—the companion with whom he had shared four winters and perhaps too many dreams—he had no longer opened his heart to anyone. He had exposed himself too much with that man, more than ever before. He only realised this later, when it was too late, and there was nothing left but to try to heal the wounds as swiftly as possible.

Davis Cooke, despite initial reassurances, ultimately could not withstand the solitude of the ranch, the long silences, the days filled with physical labour, wind, and snow. In any case, he had always been too ambitious to remain and adapt to life in the small town where he had been born and raised. He aimed to become a partner in a large law firm, and if he stayed in Aspen Creek, he would never achieve that.

So, he had given him a sort of "ultimatum"; above all, he had made it clear that he would not endure another winter at "Silver Pine".

'I'm sorry, Chase, but I can't stay here any longer. I love you, you know, but I risk going crazy if I remain cut off from the rest of the world. I'll never be able to genuinely turn my career around here.' Sighing, he shook his head. And Chase realised he wouldn't change his mind and wouldn't be able to hold him back. 'So either you leave this place and come with me, or...'

Or it was over. Davis had left the sentence hanging, but that was exactly the point. Chase understood it immediately, without being too shocked. Perhaps, after all, he'd expected it. He knew it would happen, sooner or later. He and Davis were too different in character; they had different ideals, perspectives, and aspirations. And passion would never be enough to strengthen their bond.

So it was truly over between them, once and for all. Without unnecessary words. Without second thoughts on Chase's part. 'Silver Pine' was part of him, and Davis hadn't understood this. Forcing him to choose was like destroying him.

Since then, Chase, despite his broken heart, had learned to rely on himself. Or at least, that's what he told himself. He had trusted Davis, despite everything. He wouldn't make the same mistake again. That's why he didn't deny himself an occasional fling, but for true love, he no longer had the time or even the space.

That morning, after putting on his heavy coat and loading a pair of snow chains into his van, he received a call from Madyson Thornton, the lively mayor of Aspen Creek, who always found a solution for everyone and everything. For her, it was a kind of mission to ensure the people around her were well and happy. She had tried countless times with him; she hated the fact that he was increasingly isolating himself, especially in recent years.

Sitting behind the wheel, he decided to answer, even though he knew Madyson would almost certainly give him something to worry about. It wasn't the first time this had happened, and he tried to accommodate her as best he could. It must be said that she was very skilled at easing his conscience and making him feel that her help was necessary. Indeed, indispensable.

'Chase, dear, how are you?'

'I'm doing my usual thing, Madyson. Good, I'd say.'

'Perfect! I need a favour. Big.' Madyson's cheerful voice rang out with the confidence of someone who wouldn't take no for an answer. Nothing new. 'No, actually, huge!'

There it was, just as always! Chase sighed as he prepared to come up with every excuse he could think of. He'd already compiled a long mental list that was more or less true. Even though his employees would be handling most of the work, as usual, everything was planned down to the last detail.

'Madyson, I'm about to go out and feed the horses. And this is just the beginning. I won't even have time to catch my breath today, I'm sorry. I also have to clean the stables, review the accounts, and organise the supplies. But I promise you, next time...'

'Next time doesn't matter. I need it today.' She interrupted him without hesitation. 'It's about Edwin Parker. He's in desperate need of help, even though he refuses to admit it. The storm is worsening, and he has a mountain of parcels to deliver for "Aspen Creek Deliveries". He'll never manage without extra support.'

Chase sighed, tilting his head towards the window. Through the fogged-up glass, he glimpsed the hazy landscape of pine trees and snow. Here, there was a new mission for Madyson Thornton. And knowing her, she definitely wouldn't refuse it.

Edwin Parker, had she said? He knew him by sight, and in any case, he had heard of him. Around town, they described him as an overly serious, precise fellow, "the guy who brings everyone Christmas". A worthy substitute for Santa Claus, in short, even if decidedly younger and more... well, better not dwell on it and not let strange ideas take hold!

He knew Edwin Parker's preferences, but he didn't see him as the type for a one-night stand. It was better to set the idea aside, as he wasn't seeking anything beyond a bit of good fun with whoever was around. At this point, he needed to dissuade Madyson from her plans, whatever they were, real or imagined.

'He doesn't strike me as the type who accepts help easily.' Just to avoid using too much vulgar language.

'I know, that's why I thought of you. You're the only one stubborn and determined enough not to let yourself get sent packing!' Madyson retorted, amused. Clearly, helping Edwin Parker had become a new challenge for her; he knew her quite well by now.

'Oh, thanks for the thought, then!' Chase snorted, rolling his eyes. 'It's comforting to know in advance what awaits me, namely, being sent to f—'

'You're welcome, dear.' Madyson interrupted, laughing contentedly. Who knows what was going through her mind? Maybe, in the end, she simply wanted to help the guy, nothing more. 'Show up to him in the morning. I told him you'll be in town to get some supplies for the ranch. And be as kind as you can.'

'You know that *kind* isn't my strong point.'

'Then pretend. You're very good at it, whenever you want.'

With that, Madyson ended the call without even giving him a chance to decline her "kind request" or say anything else. Chase was silent for a moment, then burst out laughing, shaking his head.

'All right, Edwin Parker, it looks like I have no choice. Let's see what kind of person you really are. Maybe I can finally loosen you up a bit!'

CHAPTER 3

By the time Chase's van arrived in front of the "Aspen Creek Deliveries" sign, it was nearly midday. The roads remained passable, but the windscreen was covered in a layer of ice that he had to scrape off several times along the way to prevent it from thickening.

Entering the building and passing through the door of the warehouse that also served as the office, he was greeted by a wave of heat and the smell of coffee mingling with the scent of cardboard from the packaging. The heart of "Aspen Creek Deliveries" was in a state of complete chaos, yet remarkably orderly: shelves piled high with packages, duct tape strewn everywhere, and a small heater crackling in the corner.

Roughly in the centre, with his sleeves rolled up and sweat beading his forehead, the man he recognised as Edwin Parker was attempting to move a box that was perhaps a little too heavy for his size. So much so that even he would have struggled a bit.

Chase paused in the doorway, watching him for a few seconds. Edwin was so busy that he didn't even notice his arrival, despite the brief ring of the bell hanging above the door. Although he'd seen him around a few times before, he now realised that Edwin Parker was different from what he'd imagined. Perhaps more fragile, but also more determined. His brown hair fell in messy locks over his forehead, and his focused gaze had a softness that contrasted with the obvious effort he made as he tried to carry the box. There was something surprising about the man, a kind of dynamism and harmony he couldn't quite describe or classify. Maybe it was just the way he was, simply himself.

'Hey...' Chase finally made his presence known, his deep voice. 'You're risking breaking your back needlessly.'

Edwin spun around, holding the box tightly in his hands.

'I can do it, I'm used to it!' he said, narrowing his eyes at him, perhaps trying to recognise him. 'Excuse me, but who...'

'I'm Chase Lewis.' He approached confidently, extending his hand with a forced smile. 'Madyson Thornton sent me. It seems you're in serious need of assistance. And, from what I can tell, she's not entirely mistaken.'

Edwin hesitated for a moment, then placed the box on the counter and shook his hand. Chase's skin was rough, warm, and the contact between them lasted a little longer than necessary.

'I hadn't asked anyone, really.'

'I figured so. But Madyson didn't seem to agree.' Chase smiled, a wry but not hostile smile. 'And anyway, I don't see anything wrong with getting help.'

Edwin examined him carefully, his commanding build certainly drawing attention. Overall, Chase Lewis was a striking figure, clad in a black jacket, muddy jeans, a two-day beard, a cowboy hat pulled low over his dark hair, and those piercing grey eyes that seemed to scrutinise the person before him. Too much, for Edwin's tastes. It was the very opposite of his world of order, labels, and delivery schedules.

'Thank you, but the point is, I do everything here in a certain way, following a specific procedure. That's why I prefer to work alone or with someone who respects my instructions,' Edwin finally replied, resigning himself to having to explain his work to the newcomer. He was a complete stranger to him. While he appreciated his willingness to help, he had to try to dissuade him, one way or another. 'Deliveries have to follow a precise order; there are times to meet, signatures to collect... In short, it's really complicated to explain, so maybe it's better to...'

'I understand,' Chase interrupted, perhaps a little too abruptly, and frowned while looking around. 'Procedure, order—it's complicated... No problem, you manage the schedules, the signatures, all your complications. I'll handle the routes, the loads, and the deliveries. I prefer manual work, though. Thinking too much is incredibly exhausting and can be harmful to your health.'

Edwin seemed hesitant to accept Chase Lewis's brisk, decisive manner. And what did he mean by 'thinking is incredibly exhausting'? Was he teasing him? Because that was just how it felt.

Could he oppose his presence? Against that unwanted invasion that, by now, he could no longer fend off? Perhaps not, but persuading him to stop on his own initiative might not be such a bad idea.

'Well, actually… it doesn't quite work like that.'

'Not yet.' Chase pursed his lips and gave him an amused look. 'But we'll make it work. You'll be surprised.'

CHAPTER 4

The morning went by amid parcels, cold weather, and small disagreements over the organisation and management of the work.

Chase, used to the rigours of manual labour, lifted and loaded boxes with remarkable energy and dexterity, moving with the instinctive confidence of someone experienced in physical work. Edwin, on the other hand, followed every step with nearly obsessive attention, checking labels, lists, and destinations.

'The precision of your handwriting is astonishing, Parker. Did you go to school to learn how to write like that?' Chase glanced admiringly at the notes in his notebook. 'You'd be surprised to learn that the world doesn't collapse if a line isn't straight or if you overflow its banks.'

'You, on the other hand, would be surprised at how much simpler everything becomes when each line is straight and the edges are clearly defined. Order matters; I'd hate not to understand my own handwriting once I've forgotten what I wrote.'

Edwin didn't even glance up. Maybe he'd overreacted, and Chase had taken it personally.

Chase, meanwhile, was laughing. A deep, hearty laugh that echoed around the warehouse walls. He definitely wouldn't be intimidated by someone too precise and overly orderly. Someone like Edwin Parker, in short.

'I like you, Parker. You've got grit, even if you seem like the type who apologises for existing even to the walls.' What was he doing? Was he flirting with him? Yeah, after all, what did he have to lose? At worst, he'd tell him to go to hell. 'You're a tough guy, for what you do. Not everyone can do it.'

Edwin blushed slightly, not replying. Inside, however, he felt an unexpected and, above all, conflicting emotion: annoyance and, at the same time, curiosity. Chase's rude and overly hasty attitude irritated him, but his manner also put him at ease in an unusual, almost disarming way. In any case, he preferred not to give him too much intimacy. He accepted his presence only because Madyson had sent him, and it seemed rude to refuse his help. And because, he was forced to admit, their strange collaboration seemed to be working, given that the delivery times had been significantly sped up and reduced.

In the afternoon, as expected, the storm started to grow stronger. Snowflakes began to fall more heavily, and the wind almost rattled the windows. Chase leaned out the door, whistling softly.

'If this keeps up, we'll be out of sight of the road in an hour. At this point, I think it's best to get ahead with the nearest deliveries and then wait for...'

'We can't stop!' Edwin shook his head, convinced. He wouldn't listen to reason. 'I still have thirteen urgent deliveries scheduled for today, and people are counting on me. You can go, of course; you'll have your own business to attend to.'

'People can wait. You're not Santa Claus, and you don't get paid enough for impossible missions.'

'That's true, but I still try to complete my tasks and meet deadlines.' Edwin looked at him seriously. 'Perhaps you don't understand. Trust is everything; it's as if there's a pact between me and the people who entrust me with their deliveries. If I stop doing my job, I don't just lose clients. I lose respect.'

Chase sighed and fell silent. Beneath that stubborn exterior, he had a clear sense he was seeing something else: fear. The fear of letting others down, the fear of not being enough for those around him and even for himself. A feeling he knew all too well and which often made him feel inadequate. Like when, at twenty, he found himself managing the ranch alone. Luckily, his employees had always proved worthy of his trust.

'All right, Parker,' he finally said, adjusting his black cowboy hat and buckling his jacket. 'Then let's get a move on and head out, aiming to deliver all thirteen of your parcels to their destinations. But this time, let's take my van. It's built for this snowy hell. I'll drive, of course. I don't leave "missions" unfinished!'

Edwin hesitated before nodding. Maybe Chase Lewis had understood. Regardless, he was still willing to help him and indulge his "madness" in trying to meet his commitments. Not everyone was capable of that.

'Thank you.'

Outside, the wind greeted them with a chilling blast. They quickly loaded up, then climbed into the vehicle, the roar of the engine breaking the white silence of the road. As they progressed, Aspen Creek became increasingly elusive around them, almost swallowed by the blizzard.

In the muted silence of the car, Edwin gazed out the windscreen at the unseen landscape. Chase drove calmly, his large hands steady on the wheel. Every now and then he glanced at him sideways, noticing how Chase bit his lip when tense, or how he clutched the thermos of coffee like a lifeline to hold on to so as not to expose himself too much.

'Have you ever stopped, Parker?' he asked finally, breaking the almost unnatural silence that had fallen between them, not just in the room around them. 'I mean, really stopped. Not to eat, sleep, go to the bathroom, wash, and do the usual things.'

Edwin frowned and cast him a sidelong look.

'I understand what you mean. But I don't think I know how to do it. So, I guess the answer to your question is no, I never stopped.'

Chase smiled, but there was a trace of melancholy in his gaze, which was all too intent on the road they were travelling.

'I thought so. Neither did I.'

'I guessed it.'

By the time they returned to the warehouse after completing all their scheduled deliveries, the storm had already reached the point of no return. Snowflakes were falling so thickly that they obscured the world around them, and the air carried that distinctive cold, icy smell.

Edwin stepped out of the van to open and then close the gate, which was slamming even louder in the wind. Chase also got out and placed a steady but gentle hand on his shoulder.

'I believe it's really time to call it a day. We've finished our mission for today. You should feel proud of yourself; you've made so many people happy.'

Edwin turned towards him, and for a moment, their gazes locked. The steel-grey eyes reflected a piercing, almost hypnotic light. He sensed something stirring within him, a faint crack in the thick wall he'd built around himself. A feeling he forced himself to suppress, to ignore.

'Yes, you're right. We'll check the last deliveries at the warehouse, then we'll go home.' He bit his lip, smiling slightly. 'Actually, you can go now. Thanks for your help; I admit I could never have done it alone. I can manage here without any problems now.'

'You're welcome! I had fun, after all, it was new for me. Anyway, it doesn't matter; I'll wait for you so I can lend a hand in closing the gate if you need it.' Chase sighed, looking like he was about to say more but instead stopped himself.

Edwin started to feel more confused. Perhaps it was just the cold or the tiredness. Or maybe it was gratitude towards him for supporting and indulging him. Or perhaps it was the beginning of something he didn't understand and wasn't ready to name yet. In any case, he was afraid of giving his feelings too much direction. So he chose to keep pushing them away, resisting with all his strength.

As the warehouse door closed behind them, the wind outside howled louder and louder, a call that few would be able to interpret.

Edwin and Chase weren't aware yet, but the storm, both outside and within them, had only just begun.

CHAPTER 5

The wind howled from outside, growing louder and louder, forcefully pressing the snow against the warehouse windows with an almost ferocious and relentless fury.

The predicted storm had finally arrived, even more intense and disruptive than anyone in Aspen Creek had imagined. The streets were now invisible, the streetlights submerged in thick flakes that fell to the ground like wild feathers.

Inside "Aspen Creek Deliveries", time seemed to stand still. The ticking of the wall clock blended with the exhausted hum of the emergency generator, which expelled a thin plume of smoke from the back. The lights flickered from time to time, as if they too were about to fail.

It hadn't taken Edwin and Chase long to realise they were stuck there, at least temporarily. In fact, once they arrived, the situation was immediately clear. So, after the initial frustration, they had no choice but to accept it and wait for the storm to subside, at least a little, before they could look for an alternative solution.

Edwin settled into a chair beside the radiator, his hands cupped around a steaming cup of tea. The steam blurred his face as he gazed out the window at the snow, trying not to dwell on the unease he felt at that moment. He hated the thought of being trapped, torn between his desire to leave and vanish. Even more irritating was the realisation that Chase had been stuck there with him because he had chosen to help him.

His mind was racing, tireless as ever, partly because he needed to distract himself from the feelings he had begun to experience, despite himself. In fact, he dreaded he might start to feel them. So he preferred to concentrate on the number of packages left to deliver in the coming hours and days. Then, he thought of the people who risked waking up on Christmas morning without the gift they had hoped for. Finally, he considered his customers, who, perhaps, might lose faith in him if he failed.

His was an invisible chain of worries that he could never break, which continued to wear him down day after day, even when the failure to fulfil his responsibilities did not strictly depend on him but on external factors, such as adverse weather conditions.

On the other side of the warehouse, Chase Lewis was arranging some sacks near the stove to block the drafts. His tall, imposing figure moved through the shadows, and he seemed utterly confident in what he was doing and what was to come, as if he had been born to face storms. Every gesture of his was measured and calm, like that of someone who had long learned that getting nervous or even angry was pointless in certain situations.

'I think the generator's fine, too,' he finally decided, wiping his hands on a cloth nearby. He actually needed to say something, just to break the silence. Edwin didn't seem the sociable sort, with his perpetually sullen expression. 'It should hold out until morning, without too many problems. I think the storm will start to ease around dawn; after that, it'll take some time to clear the roads anyway.'

'Until morning...' Edwin glanced up at the clock on the wall. He was close to losing his mind waiting. 'Damn, it's only eight o'clock in the evening!'

'Yes. We've got a long night ahead of us.'

'But I believe the predictions are exaggerated. It may stop soon, so perhaps we'll be able to...'

'No, Parker. The forecasts aren't wrong; you know that well. So there's no point in getting your hopes up; we'll stay here until tomorrow morning, if we're lucky. Just accept the reality, especially since you can't fight against nature.'

'Oh, shit...' Edwin snorted, rolling his eyes. Of course, he'd realised the situation too, even if he didn't want to admit it, not even to himself.

Chase pursed his lips, took off his cowboy hat, and ran a hand through his dark hair, still slightly damp from the snow.

'Do you have anything to eat, or should we start munching through the boxes and undelivered goods for something edible?'

Edwin chuckled softly, a smile briefly easing his tense features.

'Besides plenty of tea and coffee, I believe I have some cereal, butter cookies, tuna, and a couple of cans of bean soup in the pantry. Maybe some sodas and even a few beers, if Tyler hasn't wiped them out all these past few days.' He sighed, resting a hand on his forehead. 'I was thinking of going to stock up on supplies, but unfortunately, I haven't had the time.'

'It doesn't matter; we'll manage with what we have.' Chase approached, then pulled out a chair and sat down beside him, resting his elbows on his knees. 'Are you cold?'

Edwin hesitated before answering. 'A little, but I'm used to it now. I can handle it.'

Chase stood up, retrieved a blanket from the couch in the corner, then returned and draped it over Edwin's shoulders without saying a word. The simple, straightforward gesture caught him by surprise. Edwin glanced at him for a moment, nodded his thanks, but said nothing. Then he turned to the window, pretending to check the snow that kept falling relentlessly around them, trapping them there.

A strange quiet settled between them, broken only by the fury of the wind. Chase fetched a cup of tea and began sipping it slowly. The warmth of the drink warmed his throat, but it wasn't enough to dispel the feeling of unease that had grown more intense over the past few hours. He couldn't tell if it was the storm or Edwin's presence that made him so tense yet, at the same time, so self-conscious. He tried to stay calm, as always, but he felt like a caged animal all the same.

He, who had long been accustomed to the sound of the wind and the comforting silence of animals, now perceived every single breath of the man with whom he shared his living space, a sound perhaps barely audible but impossible to ignore, and which was beginning to stir something inside him, a part of himself that he had recently preferred to ignore.

Edwin moved in a deliberate, almost shy manner; he rarely flinched, and most of the time, he spoke with the calmness of someone who carefully considered every word before uttering it. As if he wished not to disturb others with his presence, or particularly with his opinions. There was a naive yet stubborn side to him, a part of his personality that rebelled and refused to yield or surrender. It was precisely this that increasingly intrigued Chase and motivated him to interact with Edwin, aiming to get to know him better. As if he wanted to tear down his protective armour at all costs.

'So...' he finally broke the silence again, saying something trivial just to hear his voice again and encourage him to respond. 'Do you often get stuck here with a stranger during a snowstorm?'

Edwin shot him a dry look.

'I'd say definitely not. I usually get stuck alone. But it's due to overwork, not a snowstorm.'

Chase chuckled, a soft, authentic laugh that filled the room.

'So you are definitely improving this time. You might not realise it yet, but I am a great companion in misfortune.'

'Oh, really? What makes you think that?'

'Hmm… let's see… Among many other things, I can tell incredible stories and light a fire… In short, these are essential skills in life, don't you think?'

'Yes, I suppose so, although we don't have a fireplace here, nor even firewood. In any case, I fear you'll soon have to add another: putting up with me.'

Edwin wanted to say something funny or witty, just to keep up with Chase. However, he wasn't entirely sure that his way of stating the obvious was anything to laugh at. He felt himself flush; he didn't even know why he'd said it. He knew he wasn't the witty type; there was no point in launching into silly improvisations that never came naturally to him.

'Well, I seem to be doing quite well so far! I'm putting up with you without too much trouble, don't you think?'

Chase winked at him, and Edwin noticed that he appeared genuinely amused and pleased, despite everything. He didn't seem to be pretending. Perhaps he hadn't realised what was really going through his mind. Just as well.

They continued having superficial conversations and moments of silence, while the storm showed no signs of relenting and the evening quickly descended into complete darkness. Even the fluorescent light, meanwhile, was growing dimmer, and the stove emitted a rhythmic crackling.

Outside, meanwhile, the world seemed to have disappeared altogether. They prepared the soup and ate it with almost exaggerated delight, as if it were one of the finest meals they had ever savoured.

A curious intimacy was growing between them, one neither could explain. A sudden and simple connection, almost as if the cold outside had helped, gradually melting the barriers between them.

Edwin watched Chase sideways, trying not to stand out too much, not to seem inappropriate, not to pique his curiosity. Above all, not to provoke reactions in him that he wouldn't know how to respond to. The man he was forced to share the evening with, and with whom he would spend the night, had a strong profile, a strong chin, and an unkempt beard that seemed to move on his face whenever he spoke. Even when he laughed. And then there were his eyes. Those eyes, which appeared to change colour, between steel grey and dark blue depending on the light, and a sincere, clear smile, like the sun melting the heaviest snowfalls.

'Do you like it here in Aspen Creek?' Edwin asked suddenly, driven by an interest he couldn't suppress. And, strangely, also by a desire to keep the conversation going, which was growing steadily. 'I mean, I know you live outside the town centre, but...'

'It's true, I mostly live within the confines of my ranch.' Chase tilted his head, studied him, then nodded confidently. 'Anyway, yes, I consider Aspen Creek my home. Although I must admit, sometimes the ranch is a bit too quiet, especially when my workers aren't around. In those times, I try not to freak out and talk to myself. But I don't always succeed. Then again, of course, there are my horses; they probably listen to me even more than people do.'

'Too quiet, you say? I envy silence.'

'Silence isn't bad, at least until it becomes deafening.' Chase narrowed his eyes slightly, as if to focus his gaze on him. 'As I was saying, I often find myself talking to horses, just to feel like I'm interacting with living beings. Although I admit that... well, to be honest, I often feel like animals actually listen to me more than humans do. That's why I appreciate them and always do everything I can to keep them safe on my ranch.'

Edwin nodded and looked down.

'I completely understand what you mean.'

Chase tilted his head in an attempt to meet his gaze.

'Are you talking to someone who doesn't answer either?'

Edwin shrugged and then offered a sad smile.

'With my conscience. Or at least what I believe my conscience to be, particularly when it reminds me that...'

He sighed and ran a hand through his hair. Their shared experience, forced by the harsh weather conditions, was beginning to take a turn that was making him nervous. But he didn't know how to stop it now that they'd started to get to know each other better. Maybe they were "overdoing it", that's all. Maybe they were rushing too far.

'What does it remind you of?' Chase's voice grew deeper, deeper than it had been since they'd met.

'I don't...' Edwin bit his lip, almost forcing himself, then shook his head. He tried to think of another topic for conversation, but nothing came to mind.

'Your conscience, Edwin? What does it remind you of?' Chase pressed, narrowing his eyes at him with an intensity that seemed to peer into his heart, his soul.

'That I'm not enough.' Edwin blurted out, unable to contain himself. 'That I'll never be enough.'

CHAPTER 6

That I am not enough.

That I will never be enough.

Those words, barely whispered by Edwin, drifted softly between them, both light and heavy. Chase was silent for a moment, then leaned back in his chair, tilting his head back and gazing at the ceiling. He didn't reply to his statement, at least not directly.

'I've been talking to a ghost for months,' he finally said. 'Someone who wasn't there any more, even though I saw him in every room of the ranch. Someone who had been gone for a long time, after all. Even before he actually did.'

Edwin looked at him silently, too afraid to interfere or voice his own opinion on the matter. Still, he wished Chase would continue. He truly hoped so because he wanted to learn more about him. Actually, everything, to be honest.

'I'm talking about my ex,' Chase continued, clearing his throat. 'Davis... nice, funny, full of energy, full of zest for life. He said he loved nature, until he truly understood what it meant to live there, to decide to stay. But we were good together, so he resisted as much as he could. Then he started asking me to move away, more and more insistently. I told him I'd think about it, but in reality... I knew full well I'd never do it. I was just leading us both on, to buy time, to avoid facing the truth. He realised it too, so one night he left. No scene of despair, no screaming. After all, we'd both known for a while that we were postponing the inevitable. And I... well, all I could do was admit that maybe it was for the best. I was building a world around something that no longer existed, but I had invested a lot in this relationship. Because before... well, for me there had only been adventures, with men and even with women with whom I had never felt a real connection, that's all.'

Edwin listened silently, not interrupting. There was something in Chase's voice that clenched his chest. Perhaps it was his calmness, his clarity in explaining and analysing a situation that must have hurt him deeply, despite his efforts to suppress and deny the pain. Yet, something in his deep voice still quivered, giving Edwin the sense of a taut thread that might snap at any moment.

'I'm sorry,' Edwin whispered, without saying anything further.

Chase shrugged.

'It happens. I've learnt that you can survive everything, even those you believed would always be part of your life. But then sometimes, at certain moments, everything resurfaces again.'

Edwin inhaled slowly, trying to ignore the pang in his chest that threatened to bring his wound back to the surface. Perhaps Chase was expecting a confession from him as well, some sort of exchange of sentimental confidences between men who might have an adventure during a snowstorm that had them trapped together in a confined space. But in reality, Edwin had understood that it was as if the rancher wanted to "free himself" from the situation, to lift a weight and move on. Whatever that "move on" entailed.

So he chose to dismiss the matter quickly, avoiding too much detail that might again label him a "loser" or a "failure". After all, Chase wasn't truly dumped; his decision was deliberate.

'At the end of a relationship, it often feels terrible, I understand. Whatever the reason. The truth is, I've stopped believing in it. I no longer delude myself; I've realised it's just a waste of time and energy. Maybe, at this stage, I wouldn't even be able to recognise anything true, real. But ultimately, I'm certain it's for the best.'

Chase watched him for a long time, keeping his eyes fixed on him.

'Maybe you don't have to acknowledge it. Maybe you just need to let it into your life and allow it to happen.'

'What if it destroys me?'

Edwin responded before considering what would have been most appropriate to say in that situation. So much so that he immediately regretted his words after uttering them. He preferred not to reveal too much of himself to that man. Not so obviously.

'Then you'll know you've truly lived. The alternative would be never to feel anything again, and I... for better or worse, I don't think that's a valid option, that's all.'

Those words, spoken in a low, steady voice, lingered in the air. Edwin didn't dare reply. He feared he had already revealed himself, despite his best efforts to hold back. And he knew he had gone too far with the rancher. Yet, soon the storm would pass, and he and Chase Lewis would reappear in reality, returning to what they were: two strangers with nothing in common. In that way, oblivion would fall over that moment of sincerity and genuine candour they shared.

The wind continued to howl fearlessly outside, while inside the warehouse everything suddenly felt warmer, more alive. More real, even.

When the lights suddenly went out, Edwin jolted. The generator emitted a final, dull gasp before falling silent.

'Oh, shit!' he muttered, fumbling for his mobile to shed some light. 'I knew this would happen. This isn't the first time this bastard has suddenly deserted me.'

'Either way, we don't want to go out in the storm,' Chase said, standing up and moving closer to the window for a better look outside. 'We'd freeze in five minutes. Not that it's much better here, but at least we have some hope of surviving.'

The darkness had become nearly complete, broken only by the sporadic glow of an emergency candle Edwin kept in a drawer. He placed it on a crate he moved closer to the couch, then sat down, pulling his blanket behind him.

'We can only hold on and hope it does not last too long.'

'Let's move the couch closer to the stove,' Chase suggested. 'It'll warm us up a little.'

Edwin nodded, then got to his feet and helped Chase move the couch. They sat down, both wrapped in blankets. The distance between them had greatly diminished. He could feel the warmth of Chase's body, his steady, even breathing.

Meanwhile, time passed slowly, marked only by the wind. When Edwin began to shiver, Chase looked at him and sighed, tilting his head slightly. Edwin saw an invitation in his gaze, but he wasn't sure how to respond, fearing he'd make a mistake or misunderstand. Maybe it wasn't a suggestive glance, maybe the rancher wasn't thinking the same thing. And, after all, he'd never been the type for one-night stands. Especially with someone who was helping him run his business, the work to which he'd dedicated his life.

Edwin tried to smile, but his lips were trembling. Chase wrapped an arm around his shoulders and pulled him close, a natural, protective gesture. Edwin's body tensed briefly; he was tempted to push him away or shift aside, but then he surrendered, finding in the man's embrace a warmth he hadn't felt in a very long time.

'Relax, Parker. I'm not going to jump you,' Chase said, turning his face towards him, and Edwin felt his warm breath brush his temple. 'Unless you want me to.'

'I don't think so, Lewis. I've heard that stories born under critical circumstances always have a dramatic outcome.'

'I agree.'

Chase's heartbeat was slow and steady, a calm, reassuring rhythm. Edwin closed his eyes, surrendering to that feeling of security that engulfed him like a silent wave. But then, moment after moment, it took hold of his heart and senses, invading them entirely.

Neither of them spoke further, as if words were now unnecessary between them and they no longer had any past to recount or to unravel. Outside, meanwhile, the storm continued to rage, but inside the warehouse, the snow and cold felt distant and surreal.

Chase looked down at Edwin and saw that his face was illuminated by the flickering candlelight, adding to an almost magical atmosphere. He noticed something in his features he hadn't seen before: not just kindness or fragility, but also a quiet strength, well hidden behind the fear of making a mistake and the bewilderment he had felt from the very beginning, ever since he had come to him offering to help. A strength that, without realising it, was drawing him ever closer. The temptation to move nearer, to kiss him, was truly irresistible. So too was the urge to go further, to caress his chest, to press his hips against him. To risk everything, in short, even rejection. Usually he didn't pass up a chance for a casual fling, especially if he sensed the person was receptive. But he had given his word to Edwin Parker, and he would keep it this time.

Edwin, though he struggled to resist, eventually released his hold and slowly moved closer to the rancher. Resting his cheek against his chest, he felt the steady rhythm of Chase's heart and wondered, for the first time in ages, whether he could trust him. Not just him, but the feelings he harboured towards him. If he could allow himself to feel something again, or if it was better to run away, escape, and forget everything as quickly as possible, once they were free to leave.

Meanwhile, the silence, broken only by their breathing, grew deeper and more intimate. The storm outside the "Aspen Creek Deliveries" warehouse was still raging, but inside those four walls, a gentle, almost imperceptible warmth was forming, perhaps destined to ignite into a fierce, consuming flame, which for now was merely held back and delayed. A warmth that perhaps no snowstorm could extinguish or even contain.

CHAPTER 7

Morning arrived and found them close together, as the warmth of their bodies helped ease the emotional and physical tension that had inevitably built up.

The storm had gradually subsided, leaving behind an eerie, almost sacred silence. The world outside "Aspen Creek Deliveries" was like a white expanse, still and shining under the first winter sun, pale and faint. Snow had covered everything: roofs, roads, trees. Even the signs seemed to have transformed into delicate, fascinating ice sculptures.

Edwin was the first to wake. He was curled up on the couch, still wrapped in the blanket he'd shared with Chase. For a moment, as he opened his eyes and looked at the ceiling, he couldn't remember where he was. He couldn't even recall the details of what had happened over the past few hours. Then he sensed the warmth of Chase's body, even before he saw him beside him, and the scenes of the previous night returned more and more vividly to his memory.

He was still asleep. That deep, vulnerable, almost innocent slumber struck him. There was a profound calm in the rancher's features that he hadn't noticed when he was awake. A sense of serene, yet almost childish, strength. Edwin found himself smiling. If he had followed his instincts, he would have caressed him, then kissed him on that perfect cheekbone, all the way down to his slightly furrowed lips. He would have even caressed his chest with his hand, going further if he thought he could, waking him up. He was dying to let go, so much so that he felt his body quiver with desire. Instead, he held back, pulling away from him completely.

He walked away and then slowly stood, trying not to wake him. He moved towards the window. Outside, the morning light reflected off the snow like thousands of tiny diamonds. Everything around appeared suspended and pure, as if, somehow, the storm that had broken outside had washed away even the shadows that had stagnated within him.

Behind him, a hoarse, still somewhat sleepy voice broke the silence.

'Hey… Good morning!'

Edwin turned around. Chase had woken up and was rubbing his eyes. His forehead was slightly furrowed with sleep, his dark hair was tousled, and he still looked numb. Yet, in the bright morning light, he appeared even more handsome. His eyes shone brighter. Edwin swallowed and averted his gaze for a moment, trying not to reveal his feelings. He absolutely didn't want the rancher to notice how he felt.

But he was compelled to look at him when Chase began speaking again.

'We're covered in snow, it seems. Christmas spirit, all to ourselves. How lucky!'

'Yeah, really!' he smiled faintly and forced himself to reply, trying to keep his voice steady. 'No fireplace, though, but we could have music if we wanted. The deliveries aren't finished yet, at least as far as I'm concerned.'

Chase nodded confidently. 'Then we'll get back to work as soon as we can. Of course, I'm not abandoning the mission. I just need some extra-strong coffee to get me back on my feet.'

Edwin looked at him, tilting his face slightly. Had he understood correctly? Was he still determined to help him after being stuck in the "Aspen Creek Deliveries" warehouse because of him? Yes, Chase Lewis's confident look left no doubt about that.

'But first we need to check the roads and make sure they're passable,' Edwin replied after a moment of confusion, trying not to get lost in thoughts that had nothing to do with work. 'If they're impassable, it'll be hard to get going again.'

'We'll think about it!' Chase rose from the couch, his movements slow but determined. 'One thing at a time. But don't worry, Parker, we'll save Christmas.'

The way he said his last name always carried a peculiar yet exciting tone: a mixture of irony and affection. Edwin pretended not to notice, but each time it seemed to stir something inside him. Something he wasn't sure he could keep under control for much longer—quite the opposite. Something that would soon make him surrender. And he was beginning to suspect that Chase had realised this and was doing so intentionally.

After a cup of hot coffee and some butter biscuits, they spent the next few hours shovelling snow in front of the warehouse and unlocking the entrance to allow the van to exit without too much hindrance.

Chase, despite the bitter cold, had started working full tilt under the pale sun. He even took off his jacket, leaving only his T-shirt and his ever-present cowboy hat. His powerful muscles tensed with every movement, as if they had been specially crafted for physical labour and constant training.

Edwin did his best to focus on his work and not stare too intently, but his mind kept betraying him, and his gaze couldn't help but keep shifting to the rancher to observe his movements. The man was truly testing his balance.

'Hey, watch out!' Chase called, grabbing him by the chest as he was about to slip on a patch of ice.

Edwin found himself pressed against him for a moment, his face barely touching his. The contact was brief, but it was enough to keep him still, his heart pounding. Chase, however, gave him a mischievous smile.

'You got distracted, Parker.' His hoarse voice made him shiver. 'You have to be careful... you risk hurting yourself. And that shouldn't happen.'

'That's not true,' Edwin stammered, feeling his cheeks grow even hotter. 'I mean, I wasn't distracted.'

'Oh, no?'

Chase wrinkled his nose and bit his lip. He was tempting him, damn it! But he couldn't give in. Not just yet.

'No.' Edwin forced himself to control his breathing and challenged him with a look. 'I slipped on the ice, it happens. Be careful too, rancher.'

'Thanks for the warning. I'll try not to slip... on the ice.'

Chase's tone had been clearly suggestive, and it would have been easy for Edwin to indulge him, to let himself go, even to the point of slipping, but towards sensations he was genuinely eager to experience with him. Instead, he merely shot him a slightly sullen look, then turned his back and resumed shovelling with more vigour. Yet, he couldn't shake the idea of discussing the matter further with Chase Lewis and discovering where all these uncharted emotions might lead them—beyond the bedroom, of course.

By late morning, they finally managed to move Chase's van after loading it with the day's deliveries. The tyres would certainly sink into the snow, but from the information circulating among residents, it seemed the road leading to the centre of Aspen Creek was passable again, at least with a suitable vehicle. Fortunately, snowploughs were busy clearing the entire area.

'We still have a significant backlog of deliveries. I don't even know how they built up like this, but I believe it has grown substantially this year compared to previous years. Unfortunately, Tyler's shoulder injury has worsened the situation. And I haven't been able to find anyone to replace him.'

'Let's just say you didn't even bother looking for someone to replace him...' Chase gave him a suggestive look. 'Maybe because you were subconsciously waiting for me!'

Edwin shook his head and rolled his eyes.

'You're always so modest! Anyway, deliveries seem to have doubled. This year, everyone's eager to send gifts here to Aspen Creek.'

'Anything wrong with gifts?'

'No, absolutely not. They give, I deliver and earn! This way, we're all happy.'

With that, Edwin got into the passenger side, holding the tablet in his hand.

'We'll make it!' Chase winked, adjusting his hat. 'That's a promise, Parker.'

Edwin sighed and nodded, attempting to sound confident. The rancher often exhibited a brash, sometimes even insolent, attitude. But he couldn't have been any different; it perfectly suited his temperament and even his physique. Or maybe Edwin was starting to admit that he himself wouldn't have wanted him any different.

'If we can cover the northern and western areas by this afternoon, perhaps...'

'Maybe you'll relax for once!' Chase concluded, resting his hands on the wheel. 'Haven't you noticed that the world hasn't ended, despite the storm? And it won't end if you're a little late with your deliveries, especially if the situation isn't your fault but a natural disaster.'

'Not yet,' Edwin muttered sternly, but a smile played across his lips.

'Not yet, do you mean you haven't noticed?'

'I mean, the world hasn't ended yet. But let's try not to deliver the Christmas presents on time! Want to tempt fate, rancher?'

'No, I would say no.'

Chase grinned and rolled his eyes. Then he swung abruptly towards him, leaning so far that he nearly invaded his living space in the cockpit. Suddenly, his gaze turned serious, and Edwin sensed a longing they both could no longer contain.

The situation was becoming truly "dangerous", even far beyond the limits he'd set for himself. So much so that Edwin was beginning to realise that joking with him was the only way he could restrain himself, to avoid giving in to his instincts towards him. But he didn't know how much longer he could resist.

He was tempted, truly tempted. But they couldn't afford to waste time, so he had to hold himself back. It would be too risky to complicate things with sex. They had a mission to complete, and time was running out. They needed to save Christmas; it was the top priority right now. He couldn't afford to lose the only person who had shown a willingness to help him. There would be time for the rest later, possibly. As long as Chase Lewis didn't retreat to his ranch and shut him out of his life.

'You're incorrigible, Parker!' Chase snorted but didn't move.

'Drive, Lewis!' Edwin nodded to urge him back to his space and start the van. Then he looked straight ahead, avoiding the rancher's disdainful glance.

'All right, boss!' Chase agreed without trying to provoke him further. Except with words. 'But we have an "unfinished business", you and I. And it's only postponed.'

CHAPTER 8

The initial deliveries were a modest but important task. The secondary roads remained partly blocked, making each house feel far away and wrapped in muffled silence.

Chase drove confidently, fortunately familiar with every bend and shortcut along Aspen Creek. Edwin, meanwhile, took care of organising the sequence of packages to be delivered, with the efficiency and order that had always distinguished him.

Meanwhile, to relieve the tension, they joked about the absurd notes that often came with gifts, the overly flashy or downright strange Christmas decorations, and the inflatable reindeer that wobbled in the wind.

'I can't believe someone put a Santa Claus on the chicken coop roof,' Chase laughed. 'I even took a picture so I wouldn't forget!'

'It'll be a good way to stop the chickens from feeling left out of the festivities,' Edwin replied confidently. 'It sounds sensible. I'd do it if I had a chicken coop.'

Meanwhile, however, he bit his lips to stop himself from bursting out laughing.

'Okay... I'll have to make up for it, with my horses and my ranch.' Chase nodded seriously. 'They must have felt *left out* all these years.'

'Ah, there you go! Now I see why you took a picture. For inspiration!'

The laughter mingled with the background music and the silence surrounding them, along the snowy streets of Aspen Creek.

Edwin couldn't remember the last time he'd felt so carefree or even so relaxed with someone, especially with someone he was attracted to. Perhaps never. Most of all, he'd never had this much fun. Not even years earlier at the start of his relationship with Marvin, a relationship that had begun and then developed under the pressure of fearing he might say or do something inappropriate that would upset his partner. With Marvin, he lived in a constant state of tension. Annoying Marvin would have meant feeling wrong and inadequate. At twenty, Edwin wasn't willing to risk it, even though just being aware of his sexual preferences, coming out to his family as gay, and dealing with the mentality of a small town in Wyoming like Aspen Creek had been a real challenge for him.

With Chase, however, he didn't feel so oppressed. Perhaps it was the pressure to complete all the deliveries on time, or maybe they were both focused on a task that, at least for the moment, kept them from dwelling on anything else. On what they might feel or desire.

But Edwin had noticed that, between one delivery and the next, the glances passing between them grew longer, and the silences less awkward. Their trust was steadily increasing, more and more with each moment. Yet every time their hands touched, whether by necessity or by mistake, a shiver quickly ran through them, subtle but undeniable.

But neither of them was willing to talk about it. Chase had even stopped bringing it up. Maybe they agreed silently after the night they spent together at the warehouse and the morning shovelling snow and organising deliveries. Or, more likely, they were afraid of disrupting the delicate balance still forming between them.

It was nearly evening when they finished most of the day's scheduled deliveries. The streets of Aspen Creek became busier with lights and decorations: wreaths on doors, ornaments of every kind scattered across gardens and windows, trees illuminated in shop windows, and the aroma of cinnamon and hot coffee drifting from the cafés.

Chase parked the van by the main square and turned off the engine. He then turned to Edwin and smiled.

'I think that's enough for today. Anyway, we deserve a break before we make the last two deliveries.'

'Would it surprise you if I told you you are right?' Edwin nodded with a finally serene smile. 'We can postpone the last two deliveries until tomorrow, since we'd actually be ahead of schedule for those. We're on track; we did a really good job today.'

'Yes, so true...' Chase sighed, his grey eyes revealing a tenderness Edwin hadn't expected. 'You managed to plan the deliveries perfectly, so we didn't waste a single moment of our valuable time. You really did a fantastic job!'

It wasn't just sweetness; it was also admiration for him.

'Thank you, but I could never have done it alone.' Edwin briefly lifted his hand towards him, then quickly withdrew it. Had he followed his instincts, he would have stroked his shoulder, then his face. And then... And then, nothing. He had to hold back, at least for now. 'Shall we go and get something to eat? I'm starving!'

'Of course! The quick sandwich we grabbed for lunch wasn't enough!' Chase laughed. 'We need to refuel urgently.'

They exchanged a look filled with something neither dared to define, then they decided to get out of the van, ready to head towards the diner that was located a short distance away.

But the magic of that moment was suddenly shattered when a familiar voice, cheerful yet sharp at the same time, sounded behind them.

'Chase... look who's here!'

Chase spun around. Standing before them, wearing a sleek dark coat and a sharp smile, was Davis Cooke.

Edwin, despite having glimpsed him only a few times before, recognised him instantly. If nothing else, it was the languid way the man's eyes had fixed on Chase and, consequently, the way the rancher had responded. Above all, it was the way his gaze had become clouded with a strange, fleeting melancholy, as if he were taking a running start to retrace their shared past.

Davis was blond, nearly as tall as Chase, and his overall appearance was meticulously polished. His blue eyes, striking yet slightly aloof, twinkled with enthusiasm and vitality. He possessed the charm of someone accustomed to being noticed, regardless of the situation, and a smile that suggested he knew exactly what he wanted and how to hurt.

'Davis...' Chase greeted him, his voice unsteady, quite different from what Edwin had become used to during the hours they'd spent with him. 'I didn't expect to find you here.'

'I recognised your van and stopped,' Davis replied in a tone that sounded almost sweet and caressing. 'I'm back in the area for Christmas, actually. Besides visiting my parents, I have a sale to finish for my law firm. But I admit, I've missed this place. You have no idea how much I've missed it.'

His tone shifted again, turning suggestive as his gaze travelled down Chase's body from head to toe.

Edwin immediately perceived the rising tension between the two men, like unresolved issues lingering between them. Chase stiffened and, for the first time, seemed to be at a loss for words, as if he had suddenly lost the vivacity, wit, and subtle humour he had shown from the outset. It was as if that man, in a matter of moments, had entirely drained his vivacity, the vital energy intrinsic to him. Davis, on the other hand, strode even closer and finally placed a hand on Chase's shoulder.

'Won't you introduce me to your new friend?' he asked, giving Edwin a searching look, yet one tinged with subtle contempt. 'Oh, wait a moment. Of course! The handyman courier from Aspen Creek!'

He recognised him. Although he hadn't said anything malicious or offensive, the tone in which he'd spoken those words was insolent, maybe even deliberately humiliating. Edwin felt his face grow hot, but he stayed silent.

It was Chase's reply that confirmed to him he had not misunderstood the man's derogatory attitude.

'Davis, don't start!' Chase snapped, pulling his hand away. 'Please!'

'Don't worry, cowboy. I was just curious.' Davis's smile deepened. 'You know, I didn't expect to find you... like this. I just wanted to see who you'd replaced me with. And now that I know...'

'I didn't replace you, Davis,' Chase replied, his eyes now cold and almost expressionless. 'And anyway, it's none of your business.'

'Don't take it personally, cowboy,' Davis chuckled, biting his well-shaped lips seductively. 'Anyway, if you need to let off steam... I'll be around for a few days. You know my number well; it's always the same. I know what you want and what you like. I bet you're holding back with your new conquest, aren't you?'

'Thank you for your kind offer, but I...'

The words caught in his throat. He wasn't indifferent, not yet. Davis had always possessed the innate ability to drive him mad in every conceivable way. And he still knew how to toy with him and his self-control, that much was clear.

'I don't think it'll last long from what I see. And from what I feel, especially.' Meanwhile, Davis's gaze shifted back to Edwin. 'Don't get your hopes up, or you'll risk serious harm.'

'I'm not,' Edwin replied promptly, shrugging. 'In fact, there's nothing between us at all.'

'It was just a piece of advice, don't take it personally.' Davis pursed his lips in a pout before turning his attention back to Chase. 'Let me hear from you, cowboy. I'll be waiting!'

So saying, he turned his back, raised a hand in greeting, and walked away to get back into his expensive car, aware of and proud that he had nipped in the bud a bond that was perhaps developing too quickly, but in a natural and spontaneous way.

Chase watched him leave, his shoulders tight and his fists clenched. Edwin observed silently, searching for the right words but unable to speak them.

'I'm sorry…' Chase spoke first.

'You don't have to apologise,' Edwin replied, trying in vain to seem calm and relaxed. 'It's none of my business. I mean, I just... ended up in this situation by accident. I'd hate to get involved, so if you'd like...' He glanced at Davis's car as it sped away, brazenly rushing past them.

'No, you're wrong,' Chase retorted, his voice hoarse with a rage he couldn't openly express. 'It's your business, because... you're here, and he tried to insult you, to denigrate you. His intentions were clear, and I... I fucking let him!'

'Chase, it's definitely not your fault!'

'It is, actually. Because I know that bastard all too well. I know how he acts when he's determined to hurt someone. He's a damn megalomaniac, a fucking narcissist! I should have stopped him, I should have...'

'Hey, Lewis.' Edwin gripped him by the shoulders, forcing him to meet his gaze, trying to convey in his voice the same affectionate, ironic tone Chase often used with him. 'It's all right, really. I wasn't offended. Besides, he didn't say anything wrong. Handling shipments and delivering messages and packages is my job. And I admit, I enjoy it, so...'

'Yes, I know. But I don't want Davis to ruin everything.'

Edwin swallowed, feeling a lump in his throat. Perhaps Chase still didn't realise that it wasn't Davis who was ruining everything, but his own distressed attitude, the way he'd reacted to his provocations.

'He can't ruin anything unless you let him.'

Chase nodded slowly, but his eyes showed a flicker of doubt, uncertainty about the decision he should make. The past had resurfaced, bringing with it the danger of falling back into that vortex that had caused him to lose his dignity and self-respect.

Along the streets of Aspen Creek, the Christmas lights twinkled and strung together festively, filling those who admired them with a sense of joy and camaraderie. But in Edwin's heart, another kind of light was beginning to dawn, one that went decisively against all his rationality, his common sense. The kind that forms when fear and desire meet and merge inexorably, so much so that he still isn't sure which of the two to indulge. Which of the two would win a battle Edwin Parker was increasingly convinced he was destined to lose. As had happened before, throughout his life. As always, after all.

CHAPTER 9

The following day, the snow began to fall again, softly and almost hesitantly, as if trying to wipe away the traces of the past. It also seemed to aim at erasing those of a present that risked pulling back too far, to a phase of existence that perhaps had never truly been left behind. Not entirely.

Aspen Creek, now approaching Christmas, was more lively than ever, with its decorated shop windows, carols echoing inside the stores, and the lights twinkling among the frozen pines. Yet, to Edwin Parker, everything felt distant, hazy, as if he were viewing those scenes through steamed glass. As if he were not part of it.

After Davis's sudden appearance, he and Chase went to the diner for a bite to eat, as planned. However, after exchanging a few words, they both remained stubbornly silent, each lost in their own thoughts that had nothing to do with the joy and connection that had developed between them. They no longer joked or teased each other, as if the spell had inevitably been broken. As if they no longer had anything worth sharing.

Then Edwin had asked the rancher to accompany him to the warehouse, and they had exchanged a quick goodbye. Edwin had come in claiming to check on the remaining deliveries, and Chase had left without insisting on staying to help. Edwin also let him know that the majority of the work was already done and that he would handle the rest himself.

The fundamental issue for Edwin had shifted. It was no longer about delivering on time, but about avoiding Chase. Avoiding crossing paths with him or even thinking about him. Because, given the circumstances, it would have been ridiculous to get involved in any kind of relationship with him. Ridiculous and damaging. And besides, with the work still to be completed, he had no time to think.

He had partly lied to Chase. All things considered, there was still a lot to do. But he had decided that, for his own sanity, it was better not to have him around. It was best not to get involved beyond the limit he had already risked crossing.

So, he had started working even more than usual. And, in this case, perhaps even more than necessary. He would arrive at the "Aspen Creek Deliveries" warehouse at dawn and stay until late at night, with only a few short breaks and often skipping mealtimes. Every meticulously planned route, every package to be delivered, had become a way for him not to think.

But inevitably, every time he closed his eyes, he still saw Davis's confident smile and Chase's gaze, that moment of hesitation, perhaps too long, which he had interpreted as a crack, as a return to the past. Like the regret of something, or rather, someone, Chase would have liked to have back in his life. It was Davis Cooke, not him. And it was clear that against someone like Davis Cooke, he was no match. Against someone like Davis Cooke, he would never be the "chosen one". So he had to resign himself. Or rather, he simply had to surrender. Walk away with dignity, as much as possible.

The truth was, he was afraid. Not so much of Chase as of himself. Afraid of exposing himself, getting involved, believing in something true and profound again, or trusting someone who might later choose someone else. It had happened before, with Marvin, and he didn't want to go through it again. He didn't want to feel the way he had after the deception and manipulation he'd endured for so long.

One thing was clear. He couldn't love halfway; it was all or nothing. Now, that burden pressed heavily on his heart, causing him too much pain to face. He preferred to keep his distance once and for all when it came to his private life. He chose to focus on work and carry on, without hesitation, following the schedule he had set to satisfy his clients.

Chase's support had been vital to him, but now he was able to proceed alone. After all, apart from Tyler's cooperation, the assistance from Madyson, his mother, and a few others, it had always been like this for him. The organisation had always been his to manage; the Aspen Creek deliveries fell under his responsibility. And Edwin was more determined than ever not to let anyone down. Especially during the festive season. Especially this time.

CHAPTER 10

At dawn on Christmas Eve, the "Aspen Creek Deliveries" warehouse buzzed with activity, filled with boxes, tapes, and checklists. Edwin moved among the shelves, forcing himself to keep working and not to give up. Although he now moved almost by inertia, with a detachment he had never truly experienced before. His hands were red and chapped from the cold, his eyes dark from limited sleep, but he carried on, undeterred.

Madyson had called him, sceptical that he intended to do it all alone.

'I understand you still have a lot to do.' Her tone was impatient. One way or another, the mayor of Aspen Creek always managed to learn everything about the town and its residents. 'I sent Chase Lewis to you, so why don't you take advantage of it? I understand you haven't asked for his help anymore because there are so few deliveries left. We both know that's not true, Edwin, you still have a lot of work to do. Why are you so stubborn?'

'I'm not stubborn. The fact is...'

'Yes, you are. You're stubborn and a control freak. You don't want to depend on anyone, but Chase is the right person for...'

'No, Madyson!' he interrupted her before she could finish her sentence. Whatever she meant, he didn't want to hear it.

Edwin snorted and rolled his eyes. It was impossible to fool Madyson; he had known that for some time now. But he definitely couldn't tell her the truth; it would have been too humiliating to admit he had no intention of competing with the rancher's ex. Especially since he was certain he'd lose. No, telling her, "I'm attracted to Chase Lewis and I don't want to risk being rejected by him" wasn't a wise choice.

'I prefer to finish deliveries myself. I can organise my work better. I can do it, you know. I've always managed!'

'I have no doubt of that, Edwin. But I don't want you to risk falling ill or feeling oppressed.' He heard her sigh indignantly. 'That damned pride of yours will eventually crush you, my dear.'

'That won't happen, Madyson. Don't worry, I know my limits and I'll be careful not to cross them.'

So, he ended the conversation and hoped he had truly finished it once and for all. Perhaps Madyson hadn't grasped the situation, or maybe she had understood all too well but didn't dare voice her suspicions. It certainly wasn't pride. In any case, Edwin knew he could only keep working non-stop for now, especially because he didn't feel like stopping to think. Above all, he had no time. He would only risk becoming even more depressed, losing his rhythm, and ruining all his efforts.

'Are you really going to do it all on your own?'

When, a few hours later, he heard that deep, hoarse voice behind him, he briefly thought he had only imagined it, as if it were an unconscious manifestation of his desires.

He was placing a rather heavy box on a shelf, and it nearly slipped from his grasp. But he managed to hold it and spun around abruptly. It was almost like a déjà vu of their first encounter. His eyes widened briefly, then closed and reopened, just to reassure himself that he wasn't dreaming.

Chase stood in the doorway of the "Aspen Creek Deliveries" warehouse, his jacket partially covered in snow and a determined look on his face. They hadn't seen or heard from each other in three days, but his gaze hadn't changed. In fact, it was back to the same one he'd known from the beginning: firm, direct, implacable.

'I don't need help any longer,' Edwin replied swiftly, turning sharply to get back to his work. He couldn't look at him; he risked appearing too weak. Above all, he risked letting him see what he truly felt in his eyes. 'I'm quite far along now. So thank you, but I'm fine on my own.'

'Oh, really?' Chase approached, his pace slow but steady. 'Then why do you look like you're about to break down, Parker? And why are you avoiding me?'

'You're wrong, Lewis. I'm fine. And I'm not avoiding you, I just have my work to do!'

'That is not true.'

Edwin sighed and came to a halt, clenched his fists, and turned back to him.

'You can't possibly understand how I feel. After just a few days, do you honestly think you know everything about me? It's never been easy being... well, being who I am and having to tell the rest of the world! But you can't possibly know that, obviously!'

'Oh, why do you think it was easy for me?' Chase quickly took the last few steps, standing right in front of him. 'Just because I chose to live without explaining myself to anyone, not caring about defining my personal choices, doesn't mean I haven't faced criticism or judgement. Isolating myself hasn't made my life easier...'

'You're right, I apologise.'

'Anyway, no, I don't think I know everything about you. But I can see it and maybe even understand it. In fact, I can see and understand how you close yourself off every time someone approaches you. How you've built walls so high that no one can get past them, reach you. But, at the same time, you... you can't even breathe in there.'

'Now you're overreacting, Chase,' Edwin snorted, rolling his eyes. He couldn't afford to give in. That's why he was forced to distance himself from him, to show him the detachment he didn't truly feel. Using everything he had to achieve it, even indifference or sarcasm. 'I just have to finish my deliveries by Christmas. It's not the first time for me, and it won't be the last. And then... well, do you want to change careers? From rancher to psychologist? Go ahead, but I have no intention of becoming one of your guinea pigs!'

'I just want to know one thing. Why did you shut yourself away from me?'

Chase's direct question made Edwin realise he hadn't even noticed his protests. Or if he had, he'd ignored them and carried on without hesitation.

'I clearly prefer to be alone.' Edwin tried to keep his composure, but he felt his voice crack. He knew he couldn't hold out much longer.

'And I, on the other hand, prefer the truth.' Chase took another step forward. 'I gave you a few days, I gave you your space, but now there's no point in continuing like this. I need answers from you. Tell me that what was developing between us meant nothing to you. Tell me you didn't feel something, too. Look at me and say it.'

'Chase...' Edwin was forced to look away, trying to prevent himself from collapsing. He couldn't, and most importantly, he didn't want to, lose his dignity.

'Look at me and say it, Parker. It's not difficult.'

Chase's voice suddenly softened, becoming gentle and almost caressing, sending a deep shiver through Edwin from head to toe. Then, that unique way of calling him 'Parker'... it drove him wilder and wilder each time.

He remained silent, avoiding his gaze. Then he merely shook his head faintly.

Chase then let out a sigh and lowered his voice.

'Davis means nothing to me. Not anymore. Not for a long time now. And his behaviour a few days ago should make it abundantly clear why we're over. One of the reasons, among many others. Now he only wants me back because he realises he can't have me any longer; he's like a spoiled child who's thrown away a toy and only shows interest again when he understands it could belong to someone else.'

'Yes, I've noticed. And maybe you're right. But he knows you, Chase,' Edwin murmured, feeling almost too exposed. 'You have a history with him, memories, a past. I, on the other hand, could be only...'

'My present,' Chase softly interrupted with genuine charm, 'You could be my present, Edwin. What I want now. What matters. If only you'd give me a chance. If only you'd take the risk of truly knowing me.'

Edwin looked at him, and for a moment, the ice gripping his heart thawed. Then he composed himself and shook his head, stepping back completely to avoid any contact that might cause him to lose control.

'I really have too much to do right now.'

Chase observed him carefully but did not push him. Then he marched purposefully towards the entrance of the "Aspen Creek Deliveries" warehouse.

'All right, I get it. You really have too much to do right now.' He bit his lip and sighed, his expression resigned, repeating his own words with the same tone. Then he shrugged and cast him one last look, his piercing grey eyes fixed on him. 'But running away won't make things easier, Edwin. After saving Aspen Creek Christmas yet again and making everyone else happy, what will become of you? Just think about it.'

CHAPTER 11

Chase's question remained unanswered.

Edwin Parker hadn't the slightest idea what would become of him after saving Aspen Creek Christmas. Not this time. Or maybe he did, without even trying to think about it. It wasn't that hard, after all.

Nothing. Absolutely nothing—that was his answer. He would simply carry on, as he always did. Without turmoil, without shocks. Without great joys but also without great sorrows. And that was more than enough, in his view. Because this way, he could hope to maintain his peaceful existence and find himself in a kind of peace, a comforting well-being.

Late Christmas Eve morning, the town of Aspen Creek was bathed in a kind of exhilarating magic, seemingly straight out of a postcard. People hurried through the streets with packages and bags, children threw snowballs, and church bells rang joyfully.

Edwin was struggling to load the van for one of the many trips he'd planned for the morning when he found himself facing a small group of people he instantly recognised. They stood there, like a small army, fearlessly ready to overcome all his resistance.

'We're here to help you, Edwin.' Madyson, of course. That woman certainly couldn't take no for an answer.

'But, I…' Edwin placed the package inside the open van and sighed in resignation.

Along with the mayor, others had also arrived: Martha Dawson, the owner of the Aspen Creek bookstore and bakery; Harry Stuart, the retired postman; and Tyler, who had decided to join the rescue mission despite his still-injured shoulder, mainly to help coordinate the efforts. The boy had brought three teammates with him who were considerably fitter. Edwin's mother, Janet, also joined the group, carrying enough food supplies to feed an army.

'We're a team now!' Madyson declared. 'We can do this.'

'Yes, we know you need help...' Martha added. 'That's why we're here!'

'We certainly can't let "Aspen Creek Deliveries" fail in its mission to save Christmas,' his mother concluded, her dark eyes narrowing slightly as she gently stroked his shoulder. 'And you really can't be so stubborn as to always want to do everything yourself, sweetheart.'

Everyone nodded confidently, leaving Edwin speechless. Then, feeling somewhat embarrassed, he managed to smile.

'I truly thank you.' He was exhausted, he knew, now more than ever. And he knew that, despite all his efforts, he wouldn't be able to deliver the gifts on time. Only a miracle could help him. 'The truth is... to even hope to get everything done, I'd have to work late into the night. And now I don't know where to start...'

'Maybe you could start with the break you deserve, after all this work,' a familiar voice replied, firm but kind. It was a voice that didn't belong to anyone in the makeshift team that had appeared before him, yet to someone who had suddenly appeared behind them.

Chase.

He was back. He hadn't given up, and this time there was no hesitation in his eyes. He carried a thermos, wore his usual cowboy hat, and wore that calm yet alluring smile that could warm and melt even the snow.

'I brought you the best coffee in town,' he said, handing him the thermos. 'Mine. So, Parker, do yourself, us, and the entire Aspen Creek community a favour. Take a damn break and then let us help you. We're your only chance of delivering the presents on time. Do you realise that?'

Edwin looked at him for a long moment, unsure. Then he turned his gaze to his mother, to Madyson, and to everyone else standing before him, waiting for his reply. And it was as if something inside him relaxed when he finally decided to give in.

'Yes, I realise that.' He had no choice but to admit it, to break down the wall that kept him confined to his stubbornness. 'I... all right, I need your help. Thanks for being here.'

CHAPTER 12

It was a race against time. The small convoy of vans and vehicles threaded through the snowy streets, laden with packages and, above all, goodwill. Edwin coordinated the deliveries with his usual precision, but with a new brightness in his eyes.

Chase sat beside him as Christmas carols played through the cabin of his van. They had agreed, almost without speaking, not to discuss personal matters, at least for now. Certainly not until their mission was over, with a proper conclusion.

But each time Edwin looked at him and smiled, something inside Chase's heart melted more and more. Just like it did at every stop they made, every address they delivered to, and with every smile and "Merry Christmas" they received.

Toward evening, when the last package had been delivered and the other members of the team had gradually withdrawn to prepare for the big Winter Festival celebration, which would take place the next day in the heart of Aspen Creek, only the two of them remained sitting inside Chase's van, in front of the gate of an isolated farmhouse. It was their last planned stop, the furthest. But it was done; they had finally managed to complete their mission.

'We have really finished,' Edwin muttered, almost incredulous. 'I can hardly believe it! I didn't think I'd get through this year.'

'And yet, here we are. Now you won't have too much to do,' Chase smiled, winking before crossing his arms over his chest. 'Let's see what excuse you come up with. I'm curious.'

'Who knows! I'm full of inventiveness!' Edwin laughed, but his eyes clouded over with emotion. He sighed, lightly biting his lip. 'Jokes aside... I don't know how to thank you. It's clear I couldn't have got through this without help. Without your help, especially!'

'You don't need to thank me.' Chase turned completely and leaned towards him. His breathing mingled with his. 'You know I didn't do this just for you.'

Edwin nodded and looked at him. He recognised that the look conveyed everything: fear, gratitude, desire, hope. And so much more. Yes, so much more that he couldn't wait to uncover.

'Yes, I think I understand. But the truth is...' He closed his eyes for a moment, swallowing hard.

'What's the truth, Edwin?' Chase grabbed him by the arms, perhaps squeezing too tightly. But he certainly wouldn't let him back down. 'I'm here, talk to me!'

'I felt manipulated, Chase. It's difficult to explain.'

'By me? Did you feel compelled to accept my help?' Chase's eyes widened slightly, his breathing becoming more laboured. 'I'm sorry, I didn't mean...'

'No, that's not what I meant. And it's not about you, but about Marvin, my ex.' Edwin placed his hand on his chest and gently stroked it until he calmed down. 'When I met him, I was young; he was older. He already knew very well who he was and what he wanted. In short, he almost forced me to come out to my family and everyone else when I didn't feel ready yet. Marvin made it almost a matter of principle, as if I weren't proud to come out as gay or to be... who I am, basically! As if I wanted to hide, out of shame. He made me feel guilty.'

'He forced you to come out, I understand,' Chase sighed, gently stroking his cheek. 'I believe it's a personal choice; it should never be forced.'

'I did it anyway. I think I finally got a load off my chest, but at the time I didn't realise it wasn't just about that circumstance...' Edwin closed his eyes for a moment, savouring the intense sensation of Chase's caress, the contact with his skin. 'Marvin's always had that attitude towards me. He always tried to convince me to satisfy his needs, making me believe I was never enough, that I always had to prove something, influencing my every decision until the end of our relationship... until he cheated on me and then left me for someone else.'

'I'm sorry, Edwin, truly...'

'The decision to open "Aspen Creek Deliveries", however, was mine alone,' Edwin interrupted, raising his voice. 'My only real choice, you could say. That's why it became so important to me. That's why I care so much about fulfilling my commitments and couldn't risk compromising everything. That's why I had *too much to do*. You understand me, right?'

'Yes, of course. I understand,' Chase said, resting his forehead against his for a moment. Then he looked into his eyes again. 'And now I can also understand your resistance, your doubts about me.'

'I think I made a mistake with you in that respect. But the truth is, I spent a long time convincing myself that feelings were a storm to be avoided, kept as far away as possible. But maybe... maybe the truth is that they are a safe haven to return to, if you find the courage to let go and believe again.'

Chase smiled before taking his face in his hands and gazing into his eyes.

'Then return to me and believe once more. Let us both have this chance. I want you, Parker, and I won't give up easily.'

Edwin didn't have time to reply as instinct took over. The gap between them disappeared instantly; he gripped him by the nape of the neck and gazed into those grey eyes that now seemed to hide hopes and dreams they could share. The kiss was slow, deep, full of promises yet to be spoken.

Around them, the world seemed to hold its breath: the snow fell more softly, the distant lights shone like stars, and for the first time Edwin didn't think about what could go wrong. He didn't think about anything specific, really. Just letting go, living. Letting himself be carried away by instinct and passion.

That night, Aspen Creek rested under a star-lit sky. In the now-empty warehouse, the "Aspen Creek Deliveries" Christmas sign flickered cheerfully.

Once back at base, Edwin and Chase sat on the front step, watching the snow fall gently, like an enchanted blanket. As Christmas night lit up the town with lights and laughter, Edwin realised that, perhaps, that had been the most important "mission" of all, at least for him: the courage to open his heart again, to feel hope, to believe in love once more. To the man beside him, Chase Lewis. The rancher who had helped him save Christmas.

CHAPTER 13

The Christmas dawn rose over Aspen Creek like a gentle caress, amid the silence of the pines and the scent of burning wood. The night of the great snowstorm was now a memory: the streets were covered in a soft white blanket, the houses sparkled with Christmas decorations, and candles were lit on the windowsills. The whole town seemed to breathe in unison, as if winter, for one day, had decided to loosen its grip and grant a respite.

When Edwin woke in his small apartment, light seeped through the curtains, casting golden reflections on the floor, and the smell of coffee filled the air. He had slept very little during the night, but for the first time in a long time, he felt light. Not only that, he also felt happy, fulfilled. Free.

The exhaustion from the past days had nearly completely faded, replaced by a new sense of peace, delicate but genuine.

He slowly got out of bed, put on a sweatshirt, and paused in front of the window. Outside, people were beginning to fill the square for the most important day of the Winter Festival. Edwin smiled, watching the children running around in their colourful scarves, the musicians preparing to tune their instruments, the artists ready to display their Christmas works, the lights twinkling beneath the freshly fallen snowflakes. Then he ran a hand through his dishevelled hair, smiling almost without realising it.

It had been a long time since he experienced that scene without feeling excluded. Even during the recent time he had spent with Marvin, he failed to feel part of the Christmas atmosphere, as if something was always missing. Perhaps tranquillity, security, but above all, trust in the person next to him.

He sighed and moved towards the kitchen, increasingly attracted by the inviting aroma of coffee. He looked around. He wasn't there. But, as he neared the counter, he saw a folded note. A few words written in a handwriting he did not recognise. Not yet.

"Made some coffee. See you later. ☺ "

Edwin smiled, trying to decipher the slightly angular handwriting, followed by a smiley face, then he half-closed his eyes. The memory of him, of the night just gone by, was etched into his mind and bones. The way he moved, kissed him, held him, caressed every inch of his body as if it were something precious, unique in the world. Someone to cherish.

His words echoed in his mind, and a shiver of pleasure coursed through him.

"I want you, Parker, and I won't give up easily."

He wanted him as well. He had wanted him intensely, from the very beginning. Maybe even before he fully realised it. From the first moment his eyes had fallen on him, when he had suddenly appeared at the door of the "Aspen Creek Deliveries" warehouse, with that proud, impulsive manner.

He wanted Chase Lewis, the rancher who had come to his rescue and helped him save Christmas at Aspen Creek. And he still wanted him, even now that their mission was accomplished. He wasn't sure about the future of their relationship, but he had decided he wouldn't give up on believing in it, on truly living it to the fullest. He would give them both this chance, just as Chase had asked.

Maybe together they could find some happiness, beyond the mistakes they'd made. Beyond the storm they'd weathered together.

CHAPTER 14

By late morning, Aspen Creek's main square had transformed into a magical scene. On the stage set up in front of City Hall, the choir sang *Silent Night*, while children handed out cookies to everyone present. Stalls selling sweets of all kinds and hot chocolate emitted a tempting aroma, and the snow-covered sky reflected the warm glow of lanterns lit along the streets.

Edwin moved through the crowd, smiling and greeting friends he recognised. Martha embraced him warmly and handed him a box of freshly baked cookies.

'For the Christmas delivery hero!'

He laughed, blushing. 'The hero was the team that helped me, not me.'

'Modest as ever,' she replied with a warm smile. 'You still need to learn how to accept compliments, Edwin. Anyway, Chase Lewis was right about you when he brought us together. You truly are a hero.'

Edwin froze, surprised. 'Chase?'

'Oh, yes. He was the one who asked us to help you yesterday. He was quite persuasive. In short, he wouldn't listen to reason even though he knew you'd resist, as indeed happened at first.'

'Ah... I thought the initiative had come from Madyson and my mother...'

'No, dear, not really.' Martha chuckled amusedly. 'I say keep an eye on that handsome boy. He might have another surprise in store for you.'

Edwin smiled, trying to seem detached, but his heart started to race. He regained composure as soon as his mother came to him, followed by Madyson, Harry, Tyler, and his friends. The great team that had saved the Christmas deliveries had just regrouped.

Shortly afterwards, the main lights of the Winter Festival were all switched on simultaneously. A chorus of enthusiastic cheers echoed through the square as the large star atop the Christmas tree lit up, casting golden reflections across the surrounding area and the people gathered there.

Edwin paused for a moment, utterly captivated by the scene. Meanwhile, the voices mingled with the ringing of festive bells, and among the crowd, he truly felt like part of something beautiful.

Then, behind him, a deep, now familiar voice murmured:

'I was looking for you, Parker.'

Chase was there, dressed in his dark jacket and cowboy hat, which he carefully adjusted on his head, gently lowering it with his hand. His imposing figure seemed even more formidable, and in his grey eyes was that calm light Edwin had come to recognise, that blend of sweetness and determination that had made him impossible to resist.

'Hi.' Edwin smiled at him, pursing his lips.

'Hi.' Chase took a few steps closer, clutching something in his hands. He seemed almost intimidated. 'I... I know it's not much, but... I wanted to give you this.'

Edwin looked down. Chase held a package wrapped in ochre paper, with a red bow and a handwritten note. The same handwriting he was learning to recognise.

'To protect you from the cold, when I am unable to do it myself.'

He opened it, his fingers trembling more from excitement than the cold. Inside, there was a scarf and a pair of woollen gloves with a white-and-blue intertwined pattern.

'You didn't make them, did you?'

'Of course I did! But with a little help from Madyson and your mom,' Chase admitted, biting his lip. 'And some amazing YouTube tutorials I've been following for a while. They're not perfect, but I've had very little time to experiment. I hope to improve with my next attempts. I wasn't even sure about giving them to you because they're so... I mean, you can see it too!'

Edwin took his hand, interrupting him. 'They're perfect to me because they're yours. They couldn't be more beautiful. Besides, I could have done much worse! I'm sorry I don't have a gift for you right now.'

'You let me help you save Christmas, that's more than enough!' Chase smiled before taking a slow breath. 'I... I didn't think I'd still feel this way. I mean... that I'd feel at home here in Aspen Creek, at the Winter Festival, and with someone I desperately want by my side. But then I realised that sometimes places don't matter, and neither do celebrations. It's the people that matter.'

Edwin smiled back and looked him in the eye. 'And who matters to you, Chase?'

'You. Especially you.'

The world suddenly seemed to pause as Edwin drew him close and kissed him on the lips, carefree. There was no longer the cold, the crowds, or the Christmas music playing in the background. Just the two of them.

It was a proper kiss, deep and liberating. Chase leaned in towards him, his hands instinctively reaching for his, and their fingers became entwined. Edwin sighed softly as their lips met and their breaths mingled.

So he felt alive, more than ever. Not as a man who had rediscovered love or passion, but as someone who, after a long time, had rediscovered himself — the part of himself he thought lost amid abandonment, betrayal, defeat, and disappointment.

Meanwhile, the snow kept falling, soft, fresh, and bright, covering them in complete silence. A silence filled with everything they had searched for: comfort, hope, love.

EPILOGUE

Three months later

The snow had melted weeks ago, gradually giving way to the soft green of the meadows and the smell of damp earth. Come spring, Aspen Creek would become a different town: the rooftops shone in the sun, the streams flowed freely, and the mountains, still partly covered in white, were reflected clearly in the lakes.

Edwin slammed the van's door shut, wiping his forehead. The sun was shining brightly, and a warm breeze ruffled his brown hair. "Aspen Creek Deliveries" was thriving, with plenty of work, even after the holidays. After the chaos of Christmas, the town community hadn't stopped supporting him; requests were still constant, and they continued to multiply, making the space feel a little cramped. So much so that, soon, he'd need to consider an alternative solution. But this time, he wasn't alone in managing all the deliveries and the commitments his business entailed. He had persuaded himself to hire a couple of extra part-time workers, in addition to Tyler.

'You're late, Parker.' Chase's voice came from behind him, hoarse and amused. 'As always!'

Edwin turned, smiling. Chase was leaning against the fence, his blue shirt rolled up at the sleeves, his trademark cowboy hat shading his eyes. He appeared more relaxed and serene than usual, stroking his chin with his signature flirtatious expression.

'You're the one who's early,' Edwin replied, crossing his arms. 'As always!'

Chase gave him a seductive, suggestive look.

'Maybe I just couldn't wait to see you again. And have you back.'

Edwin blushed at the thought and didn't flinch when Chase approached, intending to grasp him by the hips and kiss him. It was a natural gesture between them, part of their daily routine, but it always managed to thrill him, to evoke that sweet, intense thrill that Chase Lewis had stirred in him since their earliest days together.

'So you read my mind, rancher.'

Over the past few months, they had gradually found a balance that became essential to their daily routines. Chase helped him with deliveries for "Aspen Creek Deliveries" when he was not busy at the ranch, and Edwin joined him on weekends to assist with the work and care for the horses and fences. They had learned to live with their differences: Edwin's meticulous, painstaking precision and Chase's improvisational, natural instinct. Surprisingly, in this way, they managed to complement each other.

'Every time the wind shifts and I feel a storm brewing...' Chase said, lifting his head to look at the clear sky. 'It reminds me of that night we were stuck in the snow. The warehouse, the cold, the two of us...'

'The generator that threatened to freeze us to death... my meagre food supplies... the blanket we shared...' Edwin added, laughing. 'Very romantic indeed, you're right!'

Chase laughed with him. 'Yeah. And I still couldn't figure out whether you were going to kill me or kiss me.'

Edwin touched his hand and rolled his eyes. 'Both, I confess! You were so stubborn and pushy! And you enjoyed teasing me!'

'I know, I still enjoy it! But that night I would have gladly ripped all your clothes off, I confess!'

'You're always that cheeky one!'

They both laughed, then stood quietly for a few moments, watching the clouds slowly drift over the mountains.

'Have you ever thought about coming to live on the ranch with me?' Chase asked, suddenly serious.

Edwin looked at him for a moment, then grinned.

'I'd say almost every day since we started being together.'

Chase hugged him from behind, drawing him close. 'Then let's make it happen, Parker.'

'But...' Edwin sighed, turning his head to meet his gaze. 'I'm sad to leave everything behind, the people who trusted me with "Aspen Creek Deliveries"... another Christmas to save, then another... It's still important to me, you know.'

'Of course, I understand how much you care! That's why I believe we could relocate a significant part of the business to the ranch, enabling us to expand and adapt to daily demands. There's plenty of storage space, and it's becoming increasingly difficult to fit everything in here. Anyway, you'll always return to base when necessary. We can rely on Tyler and the guys to help; they've really proved themselves capable recently. So, don't worry, we'll save next Christmas and the one after that...' Chase smiled, pulling him close and softly kissing him.

'You see, Parker, there's a solution to nearly every problem, I suppose...'

'Yes, of course, Lewis. Apart from your knitting!'

'But those aren't just problems. They're epic disasters that even the Aspen Creek Knitting Club can't fix! But I'm having too much fun to give up. And I'm also enjoying driving your mom and Madyson crazy trying to fix my messes, so... I'll keep going!'

Edwin closed his eyes, allowing himself to be soothed by the warmth of the embrace of the man with whom, day after day, he grew more and more in love. Now he was no longer afraid of change, nor of remaining still. Above all, he was no longer afraid to expose himself, to take risks. He had found his place, and it wasn't a specific spot to live, but the arms of someone who had truly seen him from the very beginning.

The gentle spring breeze carried the distant sound of the river, singing birds, and joyful laughter that filled the air.

Winter had ended. Beneath the bright Wyoming sky, the love between Edwin Parker and his rancher, Chase Lewis, continued to flourish day after day, like that early spring that had once again brought them together.

About the author:

Facebook: https://www.facebook.com/justicewilloughbyauthor

Instagram: https://www.instagram.com/justicewilloughbyauthor